THIS CANDLEWICK BOOK BELONGS TO:

_____

_____

_____

_____

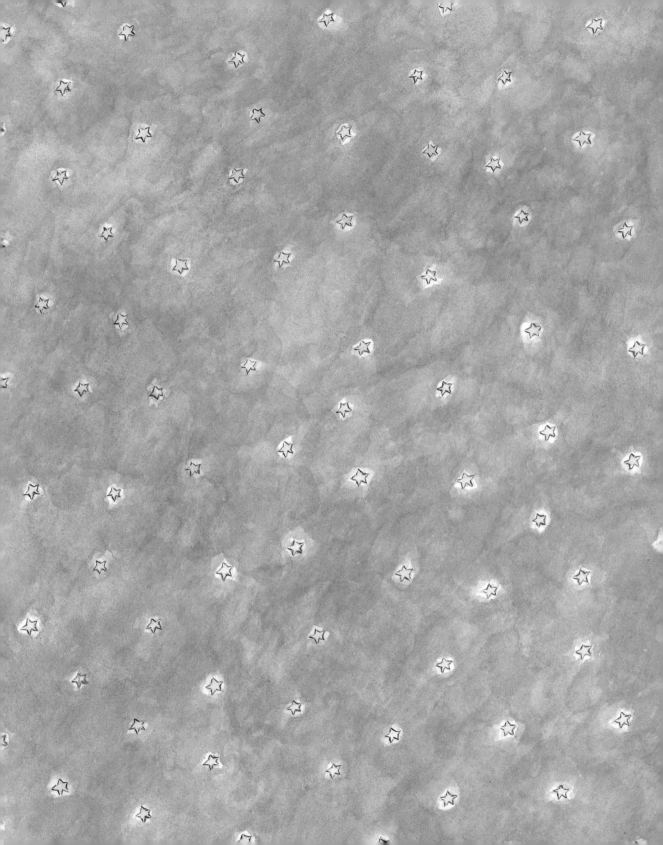

*For Laura and Harry and Tilly*
M. W.

*For Frances*
T. M.

Text copyright © 1991 by Martin Waddell
Illustrations copyright © 1991 by Terry Milne
Cover illustration copyright © 1999 by Terry Milne

First U.S. paperback edition 1999

The Library of Congress has cataloged the hardcover edition as follows:

Waddell, Martin.
The toymaker : a story in two parts / Martin Waddell ; illustrated by Terry
Milne.—1st U.S. ed.
Summary: Because Mary is too sick·to play outside with her friends, her father
makes her three dolls who are just like them; years later, as an old woman, Mary
rediscovers the dolls and finds that her father's gifts live on.
ISBN 1-56402-103-3 (hardcover)
[1. Dolls—Fiction. 2. Sick—Fiction.] I.  Milne, Terry, date. ill.  II. Title.
PZ7.W1137To    1992
[E]—dc20    91-58762

ISBN 0-7636-0705-3 (paperback)

2 4 6 8 10 9 7 5 3 1

Printed in Hong Kong

This book was set in Goudy Old Style.
The pictures were done in watercolor and pen and ink.

Candlewick Press
2067 Massachusetts Avenue
Cambridge, Massachusetts 02140

# THE TOYMAKER

## A Story in Two Parts

BY

## MARTIN WADDELL

ILLUSTRATED BY

## TERRY MILNE

CANDLEWICK PRESS
CAMBRIDGE, MASSACHUSETTS

1 Once upon a time there was a toymaker named Matthew. He loved making toys. He worked hard all day long, tap-tap-tapping and stitch-stitch-stitching. He sold the toys he made to people who came to his shop, so that he could make money to support himself and his daughter, Mary.

Mary was not strong.
She could not go out to play with
the other children.
She stayed inside and watched
them through the shop window.
Sometimes she was lonely.

Matthew wanted to make her happy
so he made her special toys.
They were dolls.
He made them very carefully,
so that each doll looked like
one of the children who played
outside the shop window.

Mary played with the dolls.
She named them Max
and Lily and Bertie,
after the children outside.
They made her happy.
Because she was happy,
she grew stronger.
At last she was able to go
outside to play.

She played and she played
and she played.
The dolls sat in the shop
window, watching.
Matthew watched, too,
as he worked.
He smiled when she laughed
because he loved her.

No one played with the dolls
anymore.
Matthew thought that Mary
had forgotten them.
He put them safely on a shelf
at the back of the shop.

People saw the dolls and asked,
"How much is this one?"
But Matthew said,
"They are not for sale.
They belong to Mary."
He would not sell the dolls,
not a single one,
for they were his memories,
and they kept him company.

 Once upon another time
an old lady came to the
toyshop with her granddaughter,
Jane. The toyshop was
empty and deserted.
"I wanted you to see it just once before it
was sold," the old lady told Jane. "This was
your great granpa's shop, where I lived
when I was a little girl."

"Was he the one who made my
  Noah's Ark?" Jane asked.
"He made lots of toys,"
  the old lady said.
"Where are they?" Jane asked,
  looking around at the dusty shelves.
"They are all gone now," said the
  old lady, and she sat still, gazing out
  through the window.

Jane went looking for toys,
just in case.
And she found some
in a dusty cupboard
at the back of the shop.

They were dolls.
She took them to the old lady,
because she didn't
want her grandmother to be sad,
and she thought the
dolls might make her smile again.

"Max and Lily and Bertie!"
the old lady said.
"They were my special toys.
I played with them here
when I was a little girl."
"Can I play with them?" Jane asked.
"I'm sure they would like that,"
the old lady said.
And Jane put the dolls in the
window of the shop, where they
could see the street outside.

An old couple passed
by the shop window.
The man stopped
and looked at the dolls.
"That's me, Lily!" he said.
"And that's me!" said his wife.
"And that's Bertie!"
They called to Bertie
to come and see.
"That's you, Bertie,"
the old man said.
"They are us,
the way we used to be."

The old people wanted
to buy the dolls and they came
into the shop and tried to persuade
the old lady to sell them.
But she said,
"They are not for sale."
And she would not sell them —
not a single one.


"But they are us!" Max said.
"You've got to sell them to us, Mary."
"I can't sell them to you,"
the old lady said.
"They belong to you already."
And she gave her old friends
the dolls that were themselves,
the way they used to be.

The old people were pleased,
but Jane wasn't.
All the dolls were gone,
and she had none left to play with.
"I'll make you a doll,"
the old lady said,
"just like the ones your
great granpa made for me!"

And she did.

She tap-tap-tapped and
stitch-stitch-stitched
very carefully
until the doll was made.

She made it with love,
for she had not forgotten.

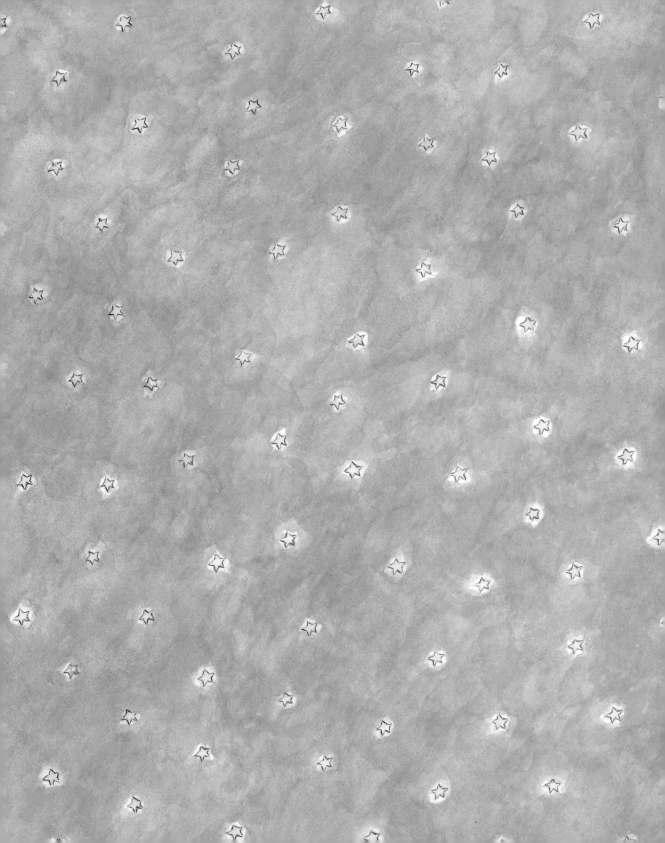

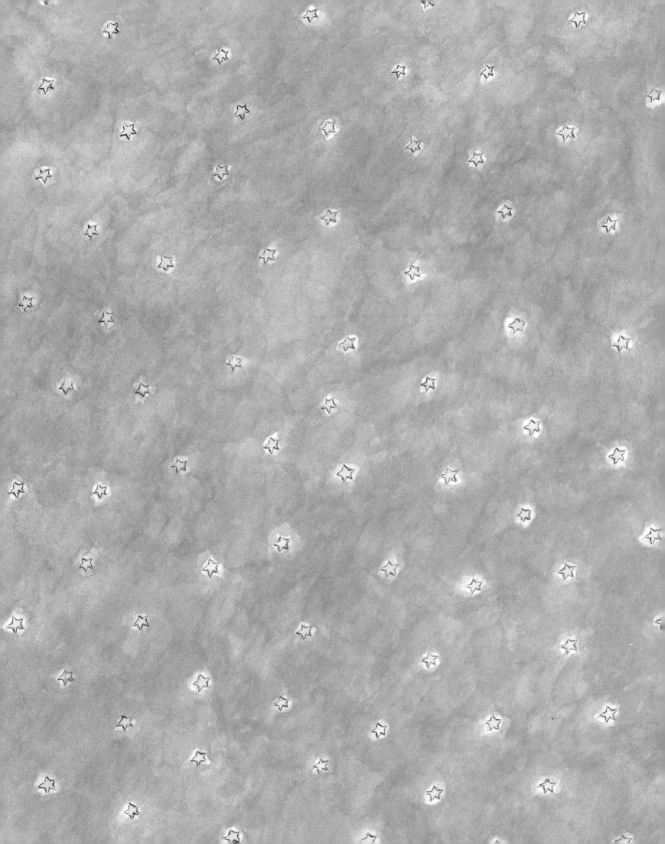

MARTIN WADDELL is one of today's most acclaimed children's book authors, with more than eighty books to his credit, including *Can't You Sleep, Little Bear?*; *You and Me, Little Bear*; *Let's Go Home, Little Bear*; *Farmer Duck*; and *Owl Babies*. Martin Waddell lives in Northern Ireland.

TERRY MILNE was born in Cape Town, South Africa. In 1989, she graduated from Stellenbosch University, where she studied book illustration. Terry Milne currently lives in South Africa.